Deserts

Ted O'Hare

Bethany, Missouri

Photo Credits:
Cover, Title Page © Photodisc; Page 5 © Andrew Nisbet; Page 6 © George Unger IV; Pages 7, 10, 11 ©
Photodisc; Page 8 © M. Lenny; Page 9 © Armin Rose; Page 12 © Seleznev Oleg; Page 13 © Nico Smit;
Page 15 © Thomas Polen; Page 16 © Norman Reid; Page 17 © Marvin Sperlin; Page 19 © Bob Kupbens;
Page 21 © Eldon Griffin; Page 22 © Stephen Coburn

Cataloging-in-Publication Data

O'Hare, Ted, 1961-
    Deserts / Ted O'Hare. — 1st ed.
    p. cm. — (Exploring habitats)

    Includes bibliographical references and index.
    Summary: Describes what deserts are, where they are found,
and what types of plants and animals live there.
    ISBN-13: 978-1-4242-1383-2 (lib. bdg. : alk. paper)
    ISBN-10: 1-4242-1383-5 (lib. bdg. : alk. paper)
    ISBN-13: 978-1-4242-1473-0 (pbk. : alk. paper)
    ISBN-10: 1-4242-1473-4 (pbk. : alk. paper)

    1. Deserts—Juvenile literature. 2. Desert ecology—Juvenile literature.
[1. Deserts. 2. Desert plants.
3. Desert animals. 4. Desert ecology. 5. Ecology.]
I. O'Hare, Ted, 1961- II. Title. III. Series.
    QH88.O43 2007
    578.754—dc22

First edition
© 2007 Fitzgerald Books
802 N. 41st Street, P.O. Box 505
Bethany, MO 64424, U.S.A.
Printed in China
Library of Congress Control Number: 2006940867

Table of Contents

What Is a Desert?

A desert is an area of land that is found somewhere on most of the world's **continents**. A desert is a **landform** that has no more than 10 inches (25 centimeters) of rainfall each year. Almost all of Saudi Arabia is desert.

Deserts cover at least one-fifth of the Earth's surface. Most deserts have high temperatures in the day but can be very cool at night. Most deserts are **arid**.

Day Temperature 100° F (35° C)

Night Temperature 40° F (5° C)

That's a difference of 60° F (30° C)

The largest hot desert in the world is the Sahara in Africa.

Some deserts, however, are always cold. The world's largest cold desert is in Antarctica.

Desert Features

Many deserts are covered with sand and have rocky **terrain**. Many of them lie in huge basins and are surrounded by mountains.

Life on the Desert

Deserts are **habitats** for animals, people, and plants. Even without much water, people and animals can live in the desert.

Desert plants can survive on very little water. Plants grow by using sunlight, soil, and water for food. **Predators** rely on these plants to keep their prey fed.

Cactuses are plants that store water. They do well in dry desert conditions.

The giant Saguaro cactus grows in the American Southwest. It provides nests for birds and is the "tree" of the desert.

Animals of all kinds, shapes, and sizes are found in the world's deserts. Many lizards and snakes live in deserts, including the gila monster. This lizard often lives alongside mountain lions and bighorn sheep.

Surviving the Heat

Many animals stay underground during the hot daylight hours. They will come out at night when it is cooler. Sometimes it gets so cold that animals, like the rock squirrel, will hide for several days.

Desert Resources

Many minerals are found in the world's deserts. These may include salt and copper. Perhaps the most valuable resource is oil, which is often found in desert conditions.

Glossary

arid (AR ud) — dry, desertlike

atmosphere (AT muh sfeer) — the character of a place

continents (KON tuh nentz) — the seven landforms that make up the Earth

habitats (HAB uh tatz) — homes for different species

landform (LAND form) — shapes and kinds of land

predators (PRED uh turz) — animals that kill other animals for food

terrain (tur RAIN) — the surface of land

Index

FURTHER READING

Davies, Nicola. *Deserts (Kingfisher Young Knowledge)*. Kingfisher Books, 2005.
Jackson, Kay. *Deserts (Earthforms)*. Bridgestone Books, 2006.
Welch, Catherine A. *Desert Plants.* Bridgestone Books, 2005.

WEBSITES TO VISIT

Because Internet links change so often, Fitzgerald Books has developed an online list of websites related to the subject of this book. This site is updated regularly. Please use this link to access the list: www.fitzgeraldbookslinks.com/eh/des

ABOUT THE AUTHOR

Ted O'Hare is an author and editor of children's nonfiction books. Ted has written over fifty children's books over the past decade. Ted has worked for many publishing houses including the Macmillan Children's Book Group.